SandCastle™

Critter Chronicles

Iguana Mama

Anders Hanson

Illustrated by C. A. Nobens

Consulting Editor, Diane Craig, M.A./Reading Specialist

ABDO
Publishing Company

Credits
Edited by: Pam Price
Curriculum Coordinator: Nancy Tuminelly
Cover and Interior Design and Production: Mighty Media
Photo Credits: ShutterStock

Library of Congress Cataloging-in-Publication Data

Hanson, Anders, 1980-
    Iguana mama / Anders Hanson; illustrated by Cheryl Ann Nobens.
        p. cm. -- (Fact & fiction. Critter chronicles)
    Summary: A newborn iguana sets out to find his mother, getting advice from other animals along the way. Alternating pages provide facts about different types of iguanas.
    ISBN 10 1-59928-444-8 (hardcover)
    ISBN 10 1-59928-445-6 (paperback)

    ISBN 13 978-1-59928-444-6 (hardcover)
    ISBN 13 978-1-59928-445-3 (paperback)
    [1. Iguanas--Fiction. 2. Animals--Infancy--Fiction. 3. Parent and child--Fiction.] I. Nobens, C. A., ill. II. Title. III. Series.

    PZ7.H1982867Igu 2007
    [E]--dc22
                                                                            2006005338

SandCastle Level: Fluent

SandCastle™ books are created by a professional team of educators, reading specialists, and content developers around five essential components—phonemic awareness, phonics, vocabulary, text comprehension, and fluency—to assist young readers as they develop reading skills and strategies and increase their general knowledge. All books are written, reviewed, and leveled for guided reading, early reading intervention, and Accelerated Reader® programs for use in shared, guided, and independent reading and writing activities to support a balanced approach to literacy instruction. The SandCastle™ series has four levels that correspond to early literacy development. The levels help teachers and parents select appropriate books for young readers.

| **Emerging Readers** | **Beginning Readers** | **Transitional Readers** | **Fluent Readers** |
| (no flags) | (1 flag) | (2 flags) | (3 flags) |

These levels are meant only as a guide. All levels are subject to change.

FACT & FICTION

This series provides early fluent readers the opportunity to develop reading comprehension strategies and increase fluency. These books are appropriate for guided, shared, and independent reading.

FACT The left-hand pages incorporate realistic photographs to enhance readers' understanding of informational text.

FICTION The right-hand pages engage readers with an entertaining, narrative story that is supported by whimsical illustrations.

The Fact and Fiction pages can be read separately to improve comprehension through questioning, predicting, making inferences, and summarizing. They can also be read side-by-side, in spreads, which encourages students to explore and examine different writing styles.

FACT OR FICTION? This fun quiz helps reinforce students' understanding of what is real and not real.

SPEED READ The text-only version of each section includes word-count rulers for fluency practice and assessment.

GLOSSARY Higher-level vocabulary and concepts are defined in the glossary.

SandCastle™ would like to hear from you.

Tell us your stories about reading this book. What was your favorite page? Was there something hard that you needed help with? Share the ups and downs of learning to read. To get posted on the ABDO Publishing Company Web site, send us an e-mail at:

sandcastle@abdopublishing.com

3

Young iguanas are independent from the start. They must find their own food and shelter.

Early one afternoon, a tiny, bright-eyed iguana hatches from its egg. "Hello, world! It's me, Kijana!" he declares cheerily. But the only reply is a shrill chirp high up in a tree.

Green iguanas spend most of their lives in trees. In Central and South America, where people eat these iguanas, they are often called chicken of the tree.

Curious, Kijana scrambles up the trunk and discovers a nest full of chicks. Kijana asks, "What are you chirping about?"

"We're waiting for our mama to come home and feed us worms," one little chick replies.

Most iguanas are herbivores. They prefer to eat plants such as fruit, flowers, and leaves.

"I'm hungry too. I wish I had a mother to feed me," Kijana says sadly.

"Don't be silly!" another chick says. "Everybody has a mama. You just haven't found her yet. Maybe you should look in the sea."

The marine iguanas of the Galapagos Islands are the only living lizards that forage in a saltwater habitat.

So little Kijana trots down to the sea
in search of his mother. But instead he
finds a baby seal barking loudly in the surf.
Kijana asks, "What's all the fuss about?"

"I'm calling my mother for help. Without
her, I might be gobbled up by a shark!"
the seal says.

If a predator attacks an iguana, the iguana may drop its tail. The detached tail wriggles and distracts the predator while the iguana runs to safety.

"I wish I had a mom
   to protect me,"
   Kijana says.

"Everybody has a
   mama. If she's not
   in the sea, maybe
   she's in the desert,"
   the seal says.

13

Iguanas are well adapted to desert life.
They can function well at temperatures up
to 115 degrees Fahrenheit.

Kijana jogs along the coast until he comes to a desert. There he meets a mother puma and her cub. Kijana asks, "Have you seen an iguana mama?"

"No," the mother puma softly replies. "But if you're missing your mama, there's a good chance that she's missing you too. Why don't you try returning to your nest?"

15

Iguanas have a third eye, called a parietal eye. It cannot see images or shapes, but it is sensitive to light.

Kijana is tired from traveling all day, but he has just enough energy to make it back to the nest. As he nears home, he sees a silhouette of a large iguana. "Mama!" Kijana shouts gleefully.

An iguana signals its mood with gestures such as head bobbing, charging, biting, and tail whipping.

Mama and Kijana greet each other
warmly by rubbing cheeks.
Mama smiles and says,
"Oh, Kijana. I'm so glad
you came home,
sweetie!"

"I thought I'd
never find
you!" Kijana
says.

19

FACT or Fiction?

Read each statement below. Then decide whether it's from the FACT section or the Fiction section!

  1. Young iguanas must find their own food and shelter.

  2. Most iguanas eat fruit, flowers, and leaves.

  3. Iguanas talk to seals.

  4. Iguanas greet each other by rubbing cheeks.

ANSWERS
1. fact 2. fact 3. fiction 4. fiction

Young iguanas are independent from the start. They   8
must find their own food and shelter.   15

Green iguanas spend most of their lives in trees. In   25
Central and South America, where people eat these   33
iguanas, they are often called chicken of the tree.   42

Most iguanas are herbivores. They prefer to eat   50
plants such as fruit, flowers, and leaves.   57

The marine iguanas of the Galapagos Islands are the   66
only living lizards that forage in a saltwater habitat.   75

If a predator attacks an iguana, the iguana may   84
drop its tail. The detached tail wriggles and distracts   93
the predator while the iguana runs to safety.   101

Iguanas are well adapted to desert life. They can   110
function well at temperatures up to 115 degrees   118
Fahrenheit.   119

Iguanas have a third eye, called a parietal eye. It   129
cannot see images or shapes, but it is sensitive to light.   140

An iguana signals its mood with gestures such as   149
head bobbing, charging, biting, and tail whipping.   156

Early one afternoon, a tiny, bright-eyed iguana hatches from its egg. "Hello, world! It's me, Kijana!" he declares cheerily. But the only reply is a shrill chirp high up in a tree.

Curious, Kijana scrambles up the trunk and discovers a nest full of chicks. Kijana asks, "What are you chirping about?"

"We're waiting for our mama to come home and feed us worms," one little chick replies.

"I'm hungry too. I wish I had a mother to feed me," Kijana says sadly.

"Don't be silly!" another chick says. "Everybody has a mama. You just haven't found her yet. Maybe you should look in the sea."

So little Kijana trots down to the sea in search of his mother. But instead he finds a baby seal barking loudly in the surf. Kijana asks, "What's all the fuss about?"

"I'm calling my mother for help. Without her,

I might be gobbled up by a shark!" the seal says. 158

"I wish I had a mom to protect me," Kijana says. 169

"Everybody has a mama. If she's not in the sea, 179
maybe she's in the desert," the seal says. 187

Kijana jogs along the coast until he comes to a 197
desert. There he meets a mother puma and her cub. 207
Kijana asks, "Have you seen an iguana mama?" 215

"No," the mother puma softly replies. "But if 223
you're missing your mama, there's a good chance 231
that she's missing you too. Why don't you try 240
returning to your nest?" 244

Kijana is tired from traveling all day, but he has 254
just enough energy to make it back to the nest. As 265
he nears home, he sees a silhouette of a large 275
iguana. "Mama!" Kijana shouts gleefully. 280

Mama and Kijana greet each other warmly by 288
rubbing cheeks. Mama smiles and says, "Oh, 295
Kijana. I'm so glad you came home, sweetie!" 303

"I thought I'd never find you!" Kijana says. 311

23

GLOSSARY

forage. to seach for food

Galapagos Islands. a series of small islands near the equator in the Pacific Ocean that are famous for their rare animals

habitat. the area or environment where a person or thing usually lives

hatchling. a baby animal that just came out of an egg

herbivore. an animal that eats mainly plants

independent. not relying on others for care or support

parietal. of or related to the top of the skull

silhouette. an outlined shape that is filled in with color or that appears dark against a light background

To see a complete list of SandCastle™ books and other nonfiction titles from ABDO Publishing Company, visit **www.abdopublishing.com** or contact us at: 4940 Viking Drive, Edina, Minnesota 55435 • 1-800-800-1312 • fax: 1-952-831-1632